★ **BOOK 2** ★

in the **Classroom 13 Series**

Disastrous

THE MAGICAL WISHES OF

CLASSROOM **13**

By **Honest Lee** & **Matthew J. Gilbert**

Art by **Joelle Dreidemy**

LITTLE, BROWN AND COMPANY

New York ✳ Boston

Little, Brown and Company
Hachette Book Group
1290 Avenue of the Americas, New York, NY 10104
Visit us at lb-kids.com

First Edition: September 2017

Little, Brown and Company is a division of Hachette Book Group, Inc.
The Little, Brown name and logo are trademarks of Hachette Book Group, Inc.

The publisher is not responsible for websites (or their content)
that are not owned by the publisher.

Library of Congress Cataloging-in-Publication Data

Names: Lee, Honest, author. | Gilbert, Matthew J., author. | Dreidemy, Joëlle, illustrator.
Title: The disastrous magical wishes of Classroom 13 / by Honest Lee & Matthew J. Gilbert ; art by Joelle Dreidemy.
Description: First Edition. | New York ; Boston : Little, Brown and Company, 2017. | Series: Classroom 13 series ; book 2 | Summary: "Ms. Linda and her students of Classroom 13 each get one wish granted from a dangerous Djinn, which brings chaos and hilarious moments to their lives"— Provided by publisher.
Identifiers: LCCN 2016038902| ISBN 9780316464543 (hardcover) | ISBN 9780316464567 (trade pbk.) | ISBN 9780316464550 (ebk.) | ISBN 9780316464529 (library ebk. edition)
Subjects: | CYAC: Wishes—Fiction. | Genies—Fiction. | Schools—Fiction. | Humorous stories.
Classification: LCC PZ7.1.L415 Dan 2017 | DDC [Fic]—dc23
LC record available at https://lccn.loc.gov/2016038902

ISBNs: 978-0-316-46454-3 (hardcover), 978-0-316-46456-7 (pbk), 978-0-316-46455-0 (ebook)

Printed in the United States of America

LSC-C

10 9 8 7 6 5 4 3 2 1

CONTENTS

Psst! Hey you. Yes, you, the reader. Earl (the class hamster) suggests using a mirror for Yuna's code. You're welcome.

CHAPTER 1
Wishless Ms. Linda

When *wishless* schoolteacher Ms. Linda LaCrosse woke up Thursday morning, she decided it would be another unfortunate day. And she was right.

First, she washed her hair with toothpaste, then brushed her teeth with shampoo and conditioner. It did *not* taste good—but her hair was minty fresh. When she got in her car, she realized it was out of gas. So she had to walk to work. On her way, the wind grew rather strong. It blew her down, and she scraped her knee. She wished that she had a wish (that would come true). But she didn't have any wishes.

I did mention she was wish*less*.

Ms. Linda was almost to work, when she noticed a giant hole in the sidewalk. It appeared that someone had been digging. *Probably mole people*, she thought.

As she was walking around the hole, a large gust of wind came along. It blew her so hard, she fell backward into the hole.

Bonk! She fell right on her bottom. Halfway buried in the rubble beside her, she saw a golden lamp.

This was not the kind of lamp you plug in to light a room. It was an ancient oil lamp that could light up a room if you filled it with oil and lit it. (An oil lamp was one of the ways people saw at night a long time ago. Of course, then some wise guy went and invented electricity and put all the oil lamps out of business.)

"What an odd place to put a lamp," Ms. Linda noted. She pulled the golden lamp out of the dirt and examined it. "It's quite beautiful, though. I'll take it to school and show my classroom. We can talk about other things one can find in the ground—rocks, worms, dinosaur bones.... Yes, what a great lesson!"

As she crawled out of the hole, Ms. Linda thought her day was starting to look up. Then, several bees started to chase her. She was only partially allergic and would not die. But bee stings still hurt. Ms. Linda knew, because bees loved to sting her. She had been stung one hundred and seventy-three times. And that was just this year.

The bees chased her all the way to the school. When she got inside, she slammed the door shut and watched all the bees bop against the glass. "Ha! You didn't get me!" Ms. Linda said. But one bee had flown ahead to wait for her inside the school. It stung her right on the lip.

"Ow! Ow! Ow!" Ms. Linda cried.

"You're late again, Ms. Linda," said the principal, pointing to his watch.

"Sawwy, Mistew Pwincipaw," Ms. Linda said. She could no longer pronounce her r's or her l's because her lip was swollen.

She rushed down the hall in her heels—*click clack, click clack, click clack*—all the way to her classroom. Her classroom was number 13, which, if you don't know, is a very *un*lucky number.

"Oh, students, I apowogize tewwibwy fow being tewwibwy wate," Ms. Linda said. "I've had quite the awfuw mowning!"

Of her twenty-seven students (including Earl the Hamster), twenty-five of them were present.

Santiago "Sniffles" Santos was not at school. He had a terrible flu. He begged his mom to let him go to school so he didn't miss anything fun, but she insisted he stay home.

William was also not in class. He had told his grandma he had a stomachache so he could stay home. But he did *not* have a stomachache. He just wanted to stay home all day and watch cartoons.

Of the twenty-five students who were in class, only twenty-two of them were awake. Of those twenty-two, seven were on their phones. Of the fifteen left, two were arguing (over something dumb) and three were drawing Jedi lightsabers (which are not dumb at all).

Of the ten students left, four were playing a card game, three were flying drones, two were studying for today's quiz, and one was running in circles. (You might think I'm talking about Earl, but I am not.)

Out of all twenty-five students present, none of them were happy to see Ms. Linda. They all *liked* Ms. Linda (especially after she gave them each a check for over a billion dollars), but they did not want to *see* Ms. Linda. Not today. Her lips were swollen to the size of two bananas, and she'd broken out into a terrible rash.

She looked quite monstrous.

"Ms. Linda!" Ava said, covering her eyes. "What happened to your face?"

"Are you turning into a zombie?" Teo asked.

"I am not tuwning into a zombie," Ms. Linda explained. "I am pawtiawwy awwewgic to bee stings, and I was stung this mowning."

"Ew," said Mya.

"Gross," said Madison.

"Votre visage est horrible!" shouted Hugo, who was from France and spoke only in French.

"That's enough, chiwdwen," Ms. Linda said. "Wet's not waste anymowe time. You'we hewe

6

to *weawn*, and I am *hewe* to teach. Today I found a *gowden wamp*."

"You mean a golden lamp," corrected Olivia.

"That's what I said, a *gowden wamp*," repeated Ms. Linda.

Ms. Linda pulled the golden lamp out of her purse. When the students saw it, they were already bored. "That lamp doesn't even have a plug," said Mark. "How's it supposed to work?"

"*Weww*, *wet* me *expwain*," Ms. Linda started. Noticing how dirty the lamp was, she gave it a hard rub with the palm of her hand. There was a loud crack of lightning and a *poof* of purple smoke—then a ghostly blue man appeared, floating in the middle of the classroom.

CHAPTER 2
Wishful Ms. Linda

Schoolteacher Ms. Linda LaCrosse and the children of Classroom 13 stared at the blue man. He was *floating* in the middle of Classroom 13 as if he were a cloud. The students could see through him a little, like a dirty window. Also, he smelled kind of bad, like a fart after eating chili for lunch.

"Um, excuse me," Ms. Linda spoke up. "Who

awe you?!" Because of her swollen lip, she still couldn't pronounce *l*'s or *r*'s.

"I am the Grand Djinn," the blue man said.

"What's a gin?" Sophia asked.

"Well, a cotton gin is a machine that separates cotton fibers from their seeds," said Olivia. She was the smartest student in the 13th Classroom.

"So you make clothes?" Sophia asked.

"No, I grant wishes," said the djinn. "I am a djinn, not a gin."

"Oh, you mean a genie!" said Ethan.

"I am *not* a genie; I am a djinn!" said the djinn. "'Genie' is a dumb word that some silly Frenchman made up while translating Arabic in the mid-seventeenth century."

"*Comment osez-vous?!*" said Hugo, offended.

"Sounds like a genie to me," said Jacob.

"I am a djinn!" the djinn thundered.

"No need to get gwumpy. Wouwd you wike a juice box?" Ms. Linda poked a straw through the foil hole and gave it to the blue man. The djinn drank it happily.

"Now, couwd you teww me why you'we hewe?" Ms. Linda asked with her swollen lip.

"I don't understand," the djinn asked. "Why are you talking funny?"

"Oh, dawn it! A bee stung me this mowning, and now I'm not tawking wight. I wish this swowwen wip wouwd go away."

"Wish granted!" the djinn said, snapping his fingers. A swirl of gold magic flew through the air and hit Ms. Linda in the lip. Her lip immediately shrank and returned to normal.

"WOW!" the whole class said in awe.

"Does Ms. Linda get more wishes?" asked Ava.

"Do all of us get wishes?" asked Teo.

"I suppose each of you can have *one* wish," the djinn said.

"Genies give three wishes!" shouted Liam.

"I am not a genie; I am a djinn. And you watch

too many movies. In the real world, a djinn only grants a person one wish. So think carefully."

Ms. Linda got very excited. She had always wanted a wish. She knew exactly what she would wish for. "As the teacher, I think I should make my wish first," she said. "That way, the students can see how to make a good wish."

"Sorry," the djinn said. "You already used your wish—on your lip."

Ms. Linda sat down and put her head on the desk. She took three deep breaths, then stood up. She would be sad later. Right now she needed to be a good teacher. "Okay, class. Listen up. Everyone gets one wish. But we will do this one student at a time. The djinn may be very cruel in not giving me another wish, but he is still a guest in our classroom. When I call your name, you can come up and tell Mr. Djinn your wish."

The kids were all buzzing with excitement. They couldn't wait for their turn.

"Oh, Mr. Djinn," Ms. Linda said. "Are there any rules the students should know about before the wishing begins?"

"Just one," the djinn said with a sly smile. "Be careful what you wish for."

CHAPTER 3
Isabella

Isabella sat all the way in the back of the classroom by the hamster, so she was often last in line. But today, by some strange stroke of good luck, she managed to be the first in line to ask the ~~genie~~ djinn for a wish—and she knew *exactly* what she wanted.

"I wish for a UNICORN!" Isabella said.

"How original," the djinn said, rolling his eyes. After a burst of magic, a unicorn appeared.

Isabella was the happiest horse-loving girl in the world...for about a day. After taking the mythical beast home, she soon realized *just how different* unicorns are from normal horses.

First, she tried to feed it. The unicorn didn't want hay or apples or carrots to eat. The unicorn became so *hangry* (hungry + angry), it smashed through the wall of her house with its sparkly horn. It destroyed her mom's kitchen, hunting for what it really wanted: fresh-baked cupcakes with pink icing and sprinkles that Isabella's mom had made that morning. The unicorn devoured them and was happy.

Isabella's mom, however, was *not*. Surrounded by complete destruction, she cried and cried. "That horned pony destroyed my fine wedding china!"

But that wasn't all.

Isabella's unicorn did not like to bathe in water. It insisted on washing itself with glitter—a *lot* of glitter. When the unicorn shook itself dry after its daily glitter bath (the same way a dog does), the entire house became coated in layers and layers of sparkly stuff as far as the eye could see.

And the thing about glitter? You can *never* get rid of it once it's in your house. Isabella's dad was *not* happy. "I can't go to work like this! My suit is coated in glitter! I look like a crafts project, not a lawyer!"

On the plus side, the unicorn did not make normal poop—*it pooped rainbows*. The colorful poop smelled like strawberry-watermelon candy, which made cleaning up sort of fun. There was never a question as to where the unicorn pooped—anyone could see the glowing rainbow pile anywhere in the house.

Stepped in poop? No problem! You're walking on rainbows the rest of the day!

That's how Isabella thought about it. Her parents—not so much.

It took a week for Isabella's parents to finally accept the unicorn as part of the family. It caused tens of thousands of dollars in property damage and ate the family goldfish. But, hey, it made Isabella happy. So her parents said she could keep it—chained and collared outside.

When Isabella was about to put the collar around the unicorn's neck, it grew wings and flew away. Unicorns are like that.

CHAPTER 4
Benji

Benji couldn't believe Isabella asked for a unicorn. That was gonna be *his* wish! He wasn't going to be a total dork and ask the ~~genie~~ djinn for the same thing. He wanted to do something original. But Benji had to rethink his wish and *fast*. After all, he was next in line.

"*Ahem*," the djinn said, growing impatient with Benji. "Are you going to make a wish or not, little man?"

"Yes!" Benji said, still thinking. "I wish for... I wish for...I wish for..."

The djinn rolled his eyes. "I wish you'd hurry up—"

Benji panicked and blurted out: "...A DINOSAUR!"

"Wish granted!" the djinn said.

✷   ✷   ✷

Taking care of a fully grown dinosaur is a lot different than caring for a new puppy or kitten or sugar glider. For starters, those animals can all fit neatly inside a shoe box. The *T. rex* was bigger than Benji's whole bedroom. So Rexy—as Benji soon named his female dino pet—stayed in the backyard.

You can imagine the neighbors' shock when they came out to water their lawn the next day. Benji's mom heard their screams and told Benji his "pet" was chasing a crowd of people down the street.

"Oops!" Benji said. "I'm sure Rexy's just chasing them with her sharp teeth in a *friendly* way. I play with my friends like that all the time."

Benji bared his teeth and pretended to stalk his mom around the kitchen. She wasn't buying it. "Train her better or she's going right back to your school, bubee."

Another difference between dinos and other pets is how they play with their owners. New kittens and parakeets form a bond with their human owners. They like that they look different. But not dinosaurs...

Any creature that wasn't another dinosaur drove Rexy into a crazed, hangry rage. Mail carriers, small animals, airplanes, you name it. Birds refused to fly over the neighborhood now—Rexy had eaten too many of them. Benji almost lost his arm the first time he tried to feed her.

"Why does Rexy have to eat *everything*?!" Benji wondered aloud.

"She's just lonely," Benji's dad said from the living room. "All her friends are dead. So she's eating her feelings."

Benji came up with an idea.

He left Rexy to chase squirrels (and a few cars) while he went to the Halloween store. "Do you have any dinosaur costumes?" he asked.

A few minutes later, Rexy stopped roaring at clouds long enough to notice another dinosaur walking up. It was teensy, but it had *Stegosaurus* plates and a spiked tail. It also wore a yarmulke. It was a *Benji-saurus*.

Rexy let out a little yip and a roar. Rexy was finally happy—she had a dinosaur playmate.

Together, *Benji-saurus* and Rexy took long walks along the beach and swam in the ocean. They played fetch, dug up yards for bones, and played hide-and-seek in the woods. (Let me tell you: Campers did not like that one.)

Benji-saurus and Rexy were great—when it

was just the two of them. Anytime other people showed up, Rexy got hangry again. Like when Benji invited Liam and Fatima over to show off his dinosaur. The moment Rexy roared, they screamed at the top of their lungs, sprinting away and waving their arms around like crazy people. Big mistake!

Rexy demolished half the neighborhood chasing after them.

Benji's mom was there to give him another warning. "Liam's parents are threatening to sue us. Get your dinosaur under control! And no dessert tonight, bubee, for either of you!"

Benji-saurus went to bed hungry that night. And so did Rexy.

"Why do you keep doing this, Rexy?" Benji asked from his window. As he stared out at the sleeping dinosaur in his backyard, he noticed his neighbor taking out the trash. Mr. Sheezenstein was his name, and he was a weirdly shaped man—he was orange from spray tan and had a square body with tiny little legs. Benji used to joke with his dad that Mr. Sheezenstein looked like a cheese cube with legs.

Mr. CHEESE-en-stein they called him (though not to his face).

Same for Liam and that dumb sweat suit he wore the other day when he came over. It was yellow sweats and a T-shirt with pepperonis all over. Liam called it his "little *slice* of cool." Everyone in class joked that it made Liam look like a walking pizza.

And that's when it dawned on Benji.

"We look like food to Rexy. That's why she's chasing us!" Benji realized.

The next day, Benji made bright neon flyers and tacked them up all over the neighborhood. Under a picture of Rexy, the flyer read:

HAVE YOU SEEN THIS DINO?

WELL, SHE'S SEEN YOU!
AND YOU LOOK LIKE FOOD TO HER!

PLEASE DO NOT WEAR ANY FOOD-THEMED CLOTHING.
(This means you, Liam.)

DO NOT BARBECUE.
(This makes you smell like hot dogs and hamburgers.)

AND DO NOT WEAR DEODORANT.
(If you smell good, she might think you taste good.)

PLEASE FOLLOW THESE SIMPLE RULES:
DON'T DRESS LIKE FOOD.
DON'T SMELL LIKE FOOD.
JUST SMELL BAD,
AND YOU'RE ALL GOOD!

Thanks,
Benji (your neighbor)

People listened and things calmed down after that. That was, until a new food truck came to town. It was shaped like a giant hot dog on wheels. As soon as Rexy saw it, she had to devour it. She chased that food truck down the highway and right out of town. Benji never saw Rexy again, but he hoped that—wherever she was—she was happy.

CHAPTER 5
Zoey

Zoey was the shortest girl in Classroom 13. How short? Well, she could wear her mom's high heels, gel her hair straight up like she'd stuck her finger in an electrical socket, stand on three or four phone books, and *still* not be as tall as Mark.

Zoey hated being short.

She wanted to get a good look at the strange

blue man, but she couldn't quite see over Benji's head. She strained, getting on her tippy-toes.

Still, no luck.

She needed to be taller. She'd always thought life would be better if she were taller: If she were, she could see over people's heads in a crowd and in movie theaters. She could finally reach the good pudding her father stashed in the high kitchen cabinet (which he never shared). And best of all, she could fulfill her dream of becoming a supermodel.

Zoey wanted to be tall and glamorous like the women in her mom's fashion magazines. And the ~~genie~~ djinn could make it happen.

When it was her turn, Zoey said, "I wish to be *taller*!"

"Wish granted, short stack!" the djinn said.

As the magic swirled all around her in a mini cyclone, Zoey could feel herself *growing*. Her fingers felt like they were stretching out of her hands. Her legs lifted her body up like she was on an elevator. And as the gold dust settled, her head bumped into the ceiling!

Zoey was now twelve feet tall.

The whole class gasped. "How's the view up there?" Liam asked. "Can you see the spitball I launched earlier?"

It was right next to her head. She could see it. It was gross. And she couldn't have been happier.

But being twelve feet tall was not as fun as Zoey thought it would be.

For starters, she could see above the heads of any crowd. But everyone stared at her. And in the movie theater, anyone sitting behind her shouted, "I can't see over your big head!"

Zoey thought some of her dad's good pudding would make her feel better. She went to the kitchen, excited to raid his hidden stash. But when she got there, she found she couldn't even squeeze into the kitchen. She was too tall.

If that wasn't bad enough, none of Zoey's clothes fit anymore. Her mom had spent a fortune buying her fancy clothes. Now they had to sew all her clothes together to make Zoey one big dress. It did *not* look pretty.

Zoey cried and cried. (And her dad *still* wouldn't share his pudding. It was almost dinnertime. He didn't want her to ruin her appetite.)

But it wasn't all bad news. The local basketball team asked her to try out. Zoey did, and she was quite good.

CHAPTER 6
William

When William woke up that morning, he didn't feel like going to school. Since his parents had run off with his fortune, he lived with his grandparents now. And they were extremely gullible. So when he told them he had a terrible stomachache, they let him stay home.

His grandma made him drink some pink liquid that tasted like chalk. As she and Grandpa left for a day of shuffleboard and Jell-O eating with friends, she said, "Call us if you need anything."

As soon as the door closed, William hopped up and did his happy dance. He did *not* have a stomachache. He turned on the TV and found a cartoon marathon. Then he started eating all the junk food in the house. By his fourth bag of chips and eighth soda and third bag of candy and second microwave pizza, he *did* have a stomachache.

He felt awful—so awful, in fact, that he puked all over himself and the TV.

TVs are not designed to withstand vomit, so it broke. His grandparents made him stay home from school for the rest of the week so they could "watch over him and nurse him back to health." That meant he didn't get to watch any cartoons.

The worst part is that he would feel even

more awful once he discovered he'd missed out on the chance to make any wish he wanted. He could have wished to never go to school again. Too bad he wasn't at school to make that wish.

CHAPTER 7
Mark

Mark—now the *second*-tallest student in Classroom 13 (after Zoey)—was very handsome. All the girls had a crush on him. But he only had eyes for one woman—Lynda Carter, an actress who once played the superhero Wonder Woman. One of the things he loved about Wonder Woman was that she flew in an invisible plane. Mark wanted to fly, too.

During class, Mark often daydreamed about what it would be like to fly above the clouds. He imagined waving at his friends from above the trees and taking naps among the birds. He wanted to zoom around the world and visit strange places.

Sometimes, he jumped off the stairs in his house just to see if he could fly. (He couldn't.)

So when the ~~genie~~ djinn came to Classroom 13 and said he would grant everyone one wish, Mark knew exactly what he would wish for. When it was finally his turn, Mark walked up to the ghostly blue wish-maker and said, "I wish I could fly."

The djinn turned him into a duck.

Now that Mark was a mallard (that's a kind of duck), Mark forgot that he was previously a human boy. He flapped his wings, took off clumsily, and flew out the window. He had to hurry if he wanted to join the other birds as they went north for the winter. Or did birds go south for the summer? Or was it west for spring break? He couldn't remember. So he just flew.

Mark ate live insects when he was hungry and pooped wherever he wanted. (Mostly on cars and on people, because even as a duck, he thought that was funny.) Though he couldn't remember Lynda Carter or being a student in Classroom 13, he *did* know that he was very happy when he was flying.

CHAPTER 8
Chloe

As Classroom 13's resident do-gooder, Chloe felt it was her duty to give her wish away. And why not? She spent all the other days of the year giving all sorts of stuff away to people or organizations that needed it more than her.

She gave canned goods to the hungry.

She donated clothes to the needy.

She mailed seeds to the seedless.

She even gifted gummy bears to the gummy-bear-less!

Chloe *cared*.

"Can I give my wish to someone else?" Chloe asked the ~~genie~~ djinn.

"Why?" the djinn asked, concerned. "No one gives away their wish. Is this a trick? Are you trying to use your wish for evil? Granting evil wishes makes me feel really crummy about my line of work."

"No!" Chloe said. "Nothing like that at all. I want to give my wish away to someone in need. It's kind of my thing."

The djinn shrugged. "Very well. Let's have it, then. Just say the words."

"I wish to give my wish away to someone else, somewhere far away, who really needs it and deserves it."

✷   ✷   ✷

At that exact moment, on the other side of the world, a young girl named Tanvi said: "I wish I had a dragon."

And *POOF!* An enormous fire-breathing dragon appeared out of thin air. Tanvi could barely believe it—a real live dragon! And it was all *hers*!

The little girl ran outside with a big smile on her face to greet her new friend.

"My name is Tanvi," the little girl said. "What's yours?"

But you see, dragons don't speak any human languages. So to him, the little girl may as well have said: "Hello, Mr. Dragon, I hope you're hungry because I'd make a great after-dinner snack."

And she did. The dragon gobbled her up.

✮　　✮　　✮

"That was a very generous thing you did," Ms. Linda said.

"Thanks," Chloe said with a smile, imagining all the good she'd done with her wish. She returned to her seat, happy to have helped someone.

CHAPTER 9
Santiago

Santiago's mom made him stay home. That's why he didn't get a wish from the Grand Djinn that day. Last time this happened, he vowed to never miss school again. Of course, as you probably know, life rarely goes according to plan. Especially where moms are concerned. Moms always get their way.

CHAPTER 10
Dev

Dev was Classroom 13's biggest gamer. Sure, other kids played games here and there, but not like Dev. He was competitive about it. For him, games were a way of life.

If it took him a whole week without sleep to beat a game, he'd do it. If discovering every hidden power-up and gem in a level meant missing his favorite TV show, so be it. He didn't care about skipping family dinners or pizza parties—those were distractions without a pause button.

Video games were the only thing that mattered.

So you can only imagine how painful *losing* a game was to Dev. And that's exactly why he'd been so moody lately. A friend of the family (who was a video game designer) gave Dev the chance to play a new game before anyone else. It was called *Teddy Bear Bashers: Space Capades.*

Dev thought he'd beat it in a week.

Instead, he was going on four and a half weeks of losing on the same exact level, over and over and over.

Dev hadn't slept. He'd barely eaten. And he smelled. Who had time for baths when ultimate teddy-bear-bashing victory was on the line?

Not Dev. He was a teddy-bear-bashing space ace. But he needed to know how to beat the final boss. How were you supposed to bash the armada of alien-teddy-bear spaceships? There were

millions of them! And when you bashed one, two more took its place. It was impossible.

When it was Dev's turn to make a wish, he said, "Yo, Djinn! How do I beat the final level of *Teddy Bear Bashers: Space Capades?*"

"That's your wish?"

Dev shook his head wildly.

"Easy," the djinn said. "Don't bash."

"*Don't* bash?" Dev said. "But it's called *Teddy Bear Bashers.*"

"If you don't bash, the enemy armada doesn't know you're there. You press up, float to the top of the screen for a little while, fly over them, and, *badda bing, badda boom,* you're at the end of the level. Game over."

Dev couldn't believe it. It was that easy? *Don't bash?!*

"But...but..."

"No buts, no nuts, no coconuts. That's game over," the djinn said. "Next!"

CHAPTER 11
Yuna

The ~~genie~~ djinn let out a long, heavy sigh, then cracked his knuckles. He was clearly annoyed.

"What's wrong?" Ms. Linda asked. "Are you still thirsty? Those juice boxes *are* rather small. Would you like something else? Lamp oil? Lamp oil with ice?"

The Grand Djinn cleared his throat. "If granting wishes for your class wasn't strange enough, this girl won't even tell me what her wish is," the blue man replied. "She keeps passing me notes that make no sense."

"Oh, you must be talking about Yuna," Ms. Linda said. "She's a mystery."

The only thing Yuna's classmates and teacher knew about her was...well, nothing. She never said a word, choosing instead to communicate only in code, like a spy. Too bad the ~~genie~~ djinn and Ms. Linda couldn't figure it out.

Here's what her note said:

I WISH FOR A SUPER-SECRET SPY MISSION. SO SECRET THAT NO ONE KNOWS ABOUT IT. NOT EVEN ME.

CHAPTER 12
Liam

Liam wasn't one to brag, but he'd accomplished a lot for a boy his age. He was undefeated in the Classroom 13 prank wars. He was one of the youngest *Global Book of World Records* record holders (for Most Powerful Fart Ever Farted by a Human Being). And just this morning, he'd had the most brilliant idea known to mankind.

Well, *mer*mankind...

"I'm going to learn how to breathe under-water for a really long time," he told his friends at the bus stop before school. "That way I can be a merman."

"Why do you want to be a merman?" Dev asked.

"Have you *seen* mermaids? They're beautiful! Plus, all mermen have perfect abs. I wouldn't even have to do sit-ups. I could just watch monster movies all day and have abs. My idea is *ABS*-so-lutely genius!"

Liam laughed and laughed at that. Dev just shook his head.

"*ABS*-so-lutely!" Liam repeated over and over. He chuckled at his own cleverness. No one found Liam's jokes funnier than Liam himself. The entire way to school that morning, it was all Liam could think about.

Liam had no idea how to learn to hold his breath underwater. But once Ms. Linda freed that ~~genie~~ djinn, he knew his wish.

★　　★　　★

Having seen a few kids' wishes backfire already, Liam should've known to choose his words carefully. It was all about phrasing with this fussy blue wish-granter. But Liam was too focused on holding in a big fart. (If he held them in, they just got bigger, which he thought was funny.)

"I wish I could breathe underwater!" Liam said.

The Grand Djinn didn't even bother to look up at him. He conjured a magical cloud out of thin air for the boy and *poof*!

Suddenly, Liam felt light-headed. His heart began to race. The world went all blurry. He felt like he couldn't breathe—probably because he couldn't.

Liam had wished to breathe underwater. He hadn't said anything about still being able to breathe air. The djinn had given him gills.

Like a fish on dry land, Liam was flailing all around, gasping for help. He needed to be submerged in water to breathe.

Luckily, Olivia—the smartest girl in Classroom 13—spotted the gills. "He needs water!" She grabbed the class fishbowl and shoved it (upside down) onto his head.

The students and teacher of Classroom 13 waited, hoping for the best....

A few seconds later, Liam opened his eyes and saw his classmates looking back at him. He smiled and waved.

"Hey, it worked! I can breathe underwater," Liam said—though no one could understand him. (Have you ever tried having a conversation underwater? It's impossible to hear anything. It just sounds like mumbles and bubbles.)

"What did he say?" Teo asked.

"Je pense qu'il a dit qu'il est comme un homme-poisson," Hugo said.

While the rest of Classroom 13 resumed their places in line for the djinn, Liam checked for the abs. He lifted his shirt and found his same old tummy.

But Liam didn't mind. Life underwater was better than abs. His fishbowl magnified everything, so real life looked way more 3-D than usual. Bonus! And Olivia didn't bother to empty the fish from the fishbowl before she shoved it onto his head. Two little goldfish swam around his face. New underwater best buds. Double bonus!

"Hello, little fish friends," Liam said, bubbles floating up on every word. "I am your new aquatic overlord. You may call me Liam the Merman! No, Aqua King! No, wait...just Liam!"

He may not have been given the abs, or a fishtail, or a magical trident, but Liam felt like a true merman. He relaxed and began to enjoy his new life "under the sea."

Having spent his wish, Ms. Linda asked him to return to his desk. Liam decided that his first act as Classroom 13's resident merman would be to finally let his fart out. (He'd been saving it up all morning.) He discovered that the fishbowl made an airtight seal around his neck, so he couldn't smell it. Triple bonus!

But everyone else could smell it. It smelled like dead fish. Everyone gagged.

"How *fart*-tastic was that?" Liam said, laughing. "Enjoy, landlubbers."

CHAPTER 13
The 13th Classroom

Classroom 13 didn't get a wish. It tried to speak up and say it wanted a wish, but the ~~genie~~ djinn and the students couldn't hear the Classroom. (As you may or may not know, 13th Classrooms are *very* quiet speakers. Mostly they just whisper.)

Filled with rage at being forgotten once again, the 13th Classroom vowed revenge (for the second time) on all of Ms. Linda's students....

CHAPTER 14
Ava

Ava is one of those rare people who is good at many things. She is beautiful, smart, and a wonderful friend. But sometimes, she was too smart for her own good. For instance, on the day the ~~genie~~ djinn came to Classroom 13, Ava was feeling particularly cunning. When the djinn said every student could have *one* wish, she knew exactly what her wish would be...

...to have *more* wishes, of course!

When it was her turn, she walked up to the djinn with her hands on her hips and a sly smile on her face. Bored of granting wishes, the djinn was picking at his fingernails. "What's your wish? Let me guess, you want a pony or superpowers?"

"No. I want something better. I wish…" Ava said, pausing for dramatic effect, "…for *unlimited* wishes."

The djinn sat up straight and smiled. "You do?"

"It's a no-brainer!" Ava said.

The rest of the students in Classroom 13 groaned. That was a great wish. They should have thought of that.

"Are you absolutely, positively certain that's what you want your wish to be?" the djinn said, as if trying to hide his excitement. This was kind of a weird reaction, but it didn't stop Ava.

"I am absolutely, positively certain that's what I want my wish to be," Ava said.

"Then say it one more time," the djinn said.

"I wish for *unlimited* wishes."

"Wish granted!" the djinn said, snapping his fingers. Gold magic and purple smoke swirled around Ava. A moment later, she turned into a ghostly blue girl and got sucked into her own golden lamp.

"What did you do?!" Ava cried, banging on the lamp to escape.

"I granted your wish and made you a djinn," the djinn explained. "You see, the only person who can have *unlimited* wishes is a djinn. Of course, a djinn doesn't get to wish anything for his- or herself. But they *do* have an unlimited amount of wishes to grant for others. You're welcome."

CHAPTER 15
Teo

Teo immediately grabbed the new golden lamp and rubbed it. The new ~~genie~~ djinn Ava popped out of the lamp in a *poof* of magic and smoke. "What do you want?" she yelled.

"I want my wish," Teo said.

"No," Ava said. "I don't want to be a djinn. I'm not granting any wishes."

"But you have to!" Teo said.

"No, I don't," Ava said, going back into her lamp. Teo rubbed the lamp again, and Ava popped out again. "Stop that!"

"Not until you grant my wish!"

"You're as annoying as a little brother," Ava said.

"And you're as annoying as an older sister," Teo said. "But you still have to grant my wish!"

Ava looked at the Grand Djinn. He nodded. "It's true. This is your new job now. You're the one who asked for unlimited wishes. Well, now you have them—for other people."

"Ugh!" Ava grumped. "Fine. What's your wish, Teo?"

"I wish to be the richest person in the world!" Like Ava, Teo was also quite smart. But he should have paid better attention to how Ava's wish backfired. He should have made certain to think of his wish phrasing perfectly.

Ava got a sly look on her face and winked at

the djinn. They both giggled. "Oh. That's an easy wish." She snapped her fingers.

Teo waited. He expected his wallet to explode with cash, or his clothes to turn into solid gold, or a chauffeur to drive up in a limo and drive him to a mansion. But none of those things happened. "Where's my money?!" Teo whined.

"You didn't say anything about money," Ava said, still giggling.

"Did you muck up my wish?" Teo growled.

"Not at all," Ava said. "You said you wanted to be rich. You didn't realize it, but you were *already* the richest person in the world—rich in *love*, from your family."

His parents and grandparents and uncles and aunts and cousins ran into the room and started hugging him and kissing him and telling him how much they loved him.

Teo pulled his hair and screamed. "I wasted my wish!"

"No takesies backsies," Ava said. She and the Grand Djinn exchanged a fist bump.

"You're going to make an excellent djinn, young lady," the Grand Djinn said.

"Thank you." Ava smiled.

CHAPTER 16
Jayden Jason

After Teo threw a tantrum about how bad his wish turned out and how it was "totally Ava's fault," Jayden Jason James (Triple J for short) wasn't taking any chances. He rubbed the Grand Djinn's lamp instead.

The sour blue man reappeared in a huff. "I'm on break! Take your wishes to my apprentice."

"Yeah, about that—we took a vote, and the class agrees we would rather *you* handle the

wishes from now on," Triple J explained. "Since you're more experienced and all. No offense, Ava."

"None taken!" Ava shouted. She stuck her tongue out at Teo and squeezed back into her lamp.

"What'll it be, kid?" the Grand Djinn asked.

Triple J took a long, deep breath. The rest of Classroom 13 was on pins and needles. They knew he would do something cool with his wish. Triple J was the most popular kid in school. The class couldn't wait to hear what ~~their~~ his wish would be.

"I wish every day was a snow day!" Triple J said.

The whole class erupted into applause. Infinite snow days?! They'd never have to come to school again! It was genius! They hoisted Triple J up on their shoulders, parading him around the room like the town hero, chanting, *"Tri-ple J! Tri-ple J! Tri-ple J!"*

Suddenly, a chill came over the room. The kids could see their breath! They ran to the windows. Outside, all they could see was white in every direction. The town was invisible, blanketed in the thickest snow they'd ever seen.

Ms. Linda turned on the news on the class TV just as a reporter said: "The National Weather Service is calling this one *Super Snow-zilla Ice-pocalypse Freeze-mageddon*—the winter storm to end all winter storms. The forecast calls for nonstop blizzards forever...and ever...*and ever*! If you go outside, you're likely to freeze instantly. That means, wherever you are, stay put."

Everyone's jaw dropped. They were snowed in—*at school*!

The Grand Djinn giggled, *poof*ing himself up a huge winter coat and a hot cocoa. "Ta-ta, kids! Enjoy the snow. I'll be in my lamp!"

In a flash of sparkles, he was gone. And so was the happy chanting for Triple J.

CHAPTER 17
Sophia

Being snowed in at school was *not* the winter wonderland Triple J had in mind when he'd made his wish. Everyone huddled together, teeth chattering, trying to stay warm.

The door to Classroom 13 opened, letting in a cold draft. Ms. Linda slammed it back shut, having returned from her pilgrimage to the school gymnasium. The unlucky teacher looked like she'd just returned from hiking Mount Everest. "I borrowed the gym parachute. Everyone crawl beneath it. Our combined body heat will help keep us warm.

"Okay, everyone in?" the teacher asked. "Olivia and Liam, this is your cue."

Olivia reluctantly pulled Liam's finger. He let out a dangerously large fart. It smelled like rotten eggs, but the gas blast was warm enough to heat the whole parachute in seconds. The kids held their noses as they warmed up.

"Whose turn is it to make their wish?" Ms. Linda asked.

It was Sophia's turn. But her hearing aids had frozen and she couldn't hear anything. It didn't matter to her. While the students worried about themselves, Sophia was more worried about the plants outside.

Sophia went to the window and saw the Classroom 13 garden covered in snow and ice.

"Oh no! The plants!"

She ran to the djinn lamp, rubbed it furiously until he came out, and said, "I wish to undo Triple J's wish."

"Done," the djinn said, snapping his fingers.

The blizzard vanished, and the plants were blooming in the sunshine. "Whew," Sophia said, relieved.

"Good job!" Ms. Linda said. "You saved the class from freezing!"

All the students hugged Sophia and patted her on the back. Her hearing aids began to thaw, just in time for Chloe to say, "I'm surprised at how you spent your wish. I thought for sure you'd use your wish to make the world a more eco-friendly place."

Sophia looked outside at the classroom garden, then thought of *all* the plants in the whole wide world.

For the rest of the day, Sophia couldn't help but wonder if she'd made a terrible mistake....

CHAPTER 18
Earl

Earl had no idea what was going on. Probably because he was a hamster, which meant he was neither excited nor unexcited to meet the djinn. As long as the djinn didn't tap on the glass of his tank like the students in Classroom 13, Earl honestly didn't care.

But when the students insisted that the hamster get a wish, the ghostly blue man shrugged and said, "Sure, why not?"

The djinn turned to the hamster and said, "You get one wish, Earl. What will it be?"

At that moment, all Earl was thinking about was sunflower seeds. So when he squeaked (in his native language of Hamsterish), he said, "I wish for sunflower seeds."

His tank was filled to brimming with sunflower seeds. Earl was very happy. If only everyone could think like Earl.

CHAPTER 19
Lily

Lily Lin was the youngest of five children in her family, and she was the only girl. This meant she had to deal with four annoying older brothers. They loved Lily, but they were only nice to her on holidays. The rest of the year, they teased her. This involved tying her shoelaces together, pulling her hair, or jumping out from behind doors and scaring her.

As it always is for the youngest kid, life at

home was no picnic for Lily Lin. But you'd never know that by talking to her.

Lily was outgoing and bold but could be quite intense. For example, during her book report on *Charlotte's Web*, she concluded that it was "unrealistic that a spider and a pig would become friends." (Ms. Linda gave her a B- and encouraged her to have a more open mind. Lily protested until Ms. Linda gave her an A.)

Today, with an opportunity to have any wish, Lily knew what she wanted—an edge over her older, stronger brothers.

Lily approached the djinn and said, "I want to be stronger."

The djinn stared at her.

"Please," Lily added.

"You must use the words 'I wish,'" the djinn explained.

"I wish."

"Now put that all together in one sentence."

"Oh. I wish to have lots and lots of muscles."

But the Grand Djinn must have had lamp oil clogging his ears because he heard Lily say "mussels." Which, though the two words sound the same, are very different.

Muscles are tissues of the body that contract to produce motion. They make people fast and strong.

Mussels are bivalve mollusks, similar to clams, that people like to eat in their seafood medley, along with other weird things that have tentacles. (Gross, right?)

With a snap of the djinn's fingers, *mussels* rained down all over Lily. She was very confused. So were the other kids.

"As the only merman in this class, this offends me!" Liam said. Though no one could understand his bubbling mumbling through the fishbowl.

Lily picked up one of the mussels and sniffed it. The salty ocean smell reminded her why her family *never* ate seafood. Gathering up the mussels, Lily stuffed them into her backpack. She walked home with a smile on her face.

Opening her backpack, the smell of the salty shellfish warmed Lily's heart. She put the mussels all around her room, rubbed them on her shoelaces, and washed her hair with them.

When her brothers got home, they went to pull her hair. But before they could touch her, she said, "Shellfish."

They froze. When they sniffed the air, they all recoiled in fear.

"We're *allergic* to shellfish!" her brothers cried. If they ate or touched shellfish, their hands would blow up like balloons, and they'd have to be rushed to the hospital.

"Then it would be best to leave me alone," Lily said. "No more teasing."

Lily was now untouchable.

She bossed her brothers around and made them wait on her hand and foot like servants. If they started to be bratty, she'd reach out as if she were going to touch them and say, "Shellfish." They'd return to being on their best behavior for her.

Sure, Lily smelled like old seafood all the time now, but it was totally worth it.

CHAPTER 20
Mason

Ask anyone in Classroom 13 about Mason, and they'll tell you he's nice, funny, great at soccer, and really strong. The one thing they won't say is that he's smart.

Because he's not.

Mason didn't understand basic math, was a horrible speller, and still thought Christopher Columbus was the first basketball player to ever walk on the moon.

(Hint: He wasn't.)

Mason could've asked the ~~genie~~ djinn for a high IQ or wished to have the best grades in school. He could've even wished to never have to do homework again. He could've wished to be transformed into a super-smart, super-strong soccer-playing machine. He could have wished for anything. The sky was the limit.

Instead Mason wished for a flashlight.

As I mentioned, he's *not* the smartest kid....

The Grand Djinn just sat there, stupefied. "Kiddo, you *are* aware I am the great and powerful djinn. Sultans have asked me for fortunes and superpowers and all manner of things beyond imagination. I've given blind men their sight back and turned whole cities into dust. And here you are, asking me for a... *flashlight?*"

"Yeah!" Mason said, totally happy with his wish. "I wish for a flashlight. But a really good one!"

The blue wish-maker twirled his pinkie and—*poof!*—a brand-new flashlight appeared in Mason's hands. It still had the price tag on it: $14.99 with tax. Available at any store.

"Woo-hoo!" Mason yelled.

That day, he went home and used his new flashlight to make shadow puppets on the wall. Then he went downstairs into his scary basement and chased all the spiders away by shining his light in every nook and cranny. After that, he pointed it at his own face, under his chin, to make funny-creepy faces to scare his mom when she least expected it.

"OoooohOhhhhOhhh!" Mason said, trying to sound like a ghost. "I'm here to haunt yooooOOUUUUuuuu...."

"Mason, go away. I'm trying to brush my teeth," his mom said, a white ring of toothpaste around her mouth.

Mason turned the flashlight off. "It's me, Mom. It's Mason. Bet you thought I was a ghost, thanks to my handy-dandy flashlight! Guess what I named him."

"Who?"

"The flashlight!"

"You named your flashlight?"

"His name is Mortimer!"

"That's nice, dear," his mom said, going back to brushing her teeth. She shut the bathroom door.

Mason took Mortimer the Flashlight everywhere. Thanks to its always-bright shine, Mason was now the *brightest* kid in school.

But he still wasn't smart.

CHAPTER 21
Hugo

*H*ugo avait hâte que ce soit son tour. Il savait déjà exactement ce qu'il allait demander. Malheureusement, il était le dernier de la file.

Pendant que les autres élèves faisaient leurs vœux, Hugo s'impatientait de plus en plus. "J'en ai assez d'attendre," dit-il à haute voix. "Je voudrais être le premier en ligne."

Le génie l'entendit et dit, "Vœu exaucé!"

Hugo disparut, puis réapparut à l'avant de la file. Il fit un grand sourire et dit, "C'est mon tour maintenant!"

"Désolé, gamin," dit le génie. "Un seul souhait par personne. C'est comme ça. Au suivant!"

CHAPTER 22
Emma

Emma Embry stepped up to make her wish but walked right past the Grand Djinn. She rubbed Ava's lamp instead.

Ava appeared, very surprised to be summoned, in a *poof*! "Did you rub my lamp by accident?" she asked.

"No, my wish is kind of a personal one," Emma whispered. "And if I have to ask a blue person to help me with it, I'd rather it be a blue person I know. No offense, Mr. Genie."

"It's DJINN!" the Grand Djinn shouted. Before his head fully disappeared back under, he added, "Don't come complaining to me if she whiffs on your wish. Silly girl!"

"I won't whiff," Ava assured Emma.

"It's about my parents," Emma said. "I wish they were...*un*-divorced."

The whole class reacted with a loud gasp. Everyone knew Emma's parents (the town's premier interior decorators), but no one knew they'd gotten divorced.

"I just saw your parents together the other day," Olivia said, confused.

"They still *work* together, but they don't live together," Emma explained. "I've been spending the week with Mom at our house and the weekends with Dad at his new apartment. I hate it."

"But isn't your dad's new place nice?" asked Isabella.

"Of course it's beautiful," Emma said. "He's a decorator. But his new place is so small. It doesn't have a lot of room to sit and cry, or lie down and wallow in despair, or walk comfortably while arguing with the divorce lawyer about what *I* want."

"That sounds awful," Benji said. A lot of the kids in the 13th Classroom gave Emma a hug.

"Let's get this fixed," Ava said. "I hereby pronounce your wish *GRANTED*. I hereby pronounce your mom and dad *husband and wife*. Again."

After school, Emma ran home to find her mom and dad together again, side by side, in the kitchen. They were even holding hands.

Emma was so happy she felt like crying. "Mom, Dad, you guys are—"

"Miserable!" her mom said.

"Honey, you don't know where Daddy's handsaw is, do you? It wasn't in the rustic Victorian steamer trunk where I usually store it," her dad said.

"Why do you need a handsaw?" Emma asked. As she got within hugging distance of her parents, she realized they weren't holding hands—they were shackled to each other by a pair of enchanted handcuffs.

"We tried gardening shears, but they weren't strong enough to cut through these chains. Just like *I told you*," her mom snapped at her dad.

"Oh, well, *excuuuuuuse* me for coming up with a logical solution to our illogical handcuff problem!" her dad snapped back.

And just like that, they were arguing about how to cut off the handcuffs. Emma did her best to ignore the shouting and hug them. "Mom, Dad, please stop fighting!"

They tried to, for Emma's sake. But it didn't

last. During dinner, they were at it again. Mom wanted to use her right arm to reach for veggies, while Dad was trying to spoon some mashed potatoes with his left. Handcuffs made eating very difficult. No one got what they wanted, so Emma's mom and dad went back for a second helping—of their argument.

Emma took turns feeding them.

"Sorry, honey," her dad said, chewing a mouthful of mashed potatoes. "Please know this has nothing to do with you."

"I'm sorry, too," her mom added, chomping down on asparagus. "I'm extra sorry."

"Well, I'm way *more* sorry than you are!" her dad yelled. And then they were fighting again.

It was becoming clear to Emma that maybe her parents *shouldn't* be back together.

The next day, Emma decided to help them. She asked their handyman neighbor to cut through the handcuffs with his chain saw. But it was no use. The cuffs were too strong for normal power tools.

"This is hopeless," her dad said.

"Being married to you is hopeless," her mom added.

Emma called a cab, and the three of them rode to a local power plant with a billboard on the outside that promised THE WORLD'S MOST POWERFUL ATOMIC LASER—AND GIFT SHOP! Her mom and dad paid the laser operator two hundred bucks to zap the cuffs off. All the laser did was heat the chains up until they glowed red.

Not even the world's most powerful atomic laser was powerful enough to cut through the djinn magic. Emma's parents survived the laser blast, but all they got was a lousy T-shirt and some minor wrist burns.

Emma's parents argued in the backseat of the cab the entire way to the diamond-cutting facility on the other side of town. Emma struggled to hear the diamond cutter over her parents' bickering. "This is not a normal drill bit," the diamond cutter said. "This will cut through diamond. This will cut anything."

But the diamond-cutting drill bit was no match for the enchanted handcuffs, either. Emma's parents went back to fighting.

"My parents were the same way," the diamond cutter told Emma. "They were much happier *after* they separated."

Emma knew the diamond cutter was right. Her parents were happier apart. She had to let go.

Emma had no idea how she was going to fix this. But she had an idea to get them to stop fighting. The cab stopped at her parents' furniture warehouse. She found two antique room dividers and brought them home. These were the kind of little walls that could be folded up and put anywhere. Movie stars used them to get dressed while other people were in the same room. But Emma had a better use for it.

At home, she unfolded the room dividers, putting them between her mom and her dad. They didn't have to see each other (except through the crack where their hands were linked), which meant they didn't fight (as much). And Emma still got to have both her parents in the same house.

She took turns feeding them mashed potatoes and asparagus. It was exhausting, but it seemed to be working fine for now. There was just one problem—what was going to happen when they had to go to the bathroom?

CHAPTER 23
Fatima

If you took a poll and asked everyone in Classroom 13 what they thought Fatima would wish for, you'd probably hear them say:

"Comic books!"

"Comics, definitely."

"I bet she asks for every comic book issue ever made."

"What he said. Comics."

"Probably every single number one issue that's ever come out—bagged and boarded, of course."

"An ant farm!" (This last one was Mason's guess. He was wrong.)

Yes, Fatima was Classroom 13's avid comic-book collector. And her wish did have something to do with comics but not how you might think.

"I wish to live inside a comic book," Fatima told the Grand Djinn.

"Done!" the djinn said as a magic tornado of gold dust whisked her away into the black-and-white pages of a comic-book world.

"Black-and-white?!" Fatima whined. "This isn't the comic I meant...."

Fatima didn't recognize her new surroundings at all. The art style looked so normal and boring, like old drawings of a normal and boring neighborhood.

Where were the wizards? Where were the

alien galaxies? Where were the superpowers and the supervillains? Where was the action?!

"Welcome!" said a cartoon boy with a round, chubby face.

Fatima noticed "Welcome!" appeared above him in a *speech bubble*—a floating cloud in comics that spelled out everything a character said.

Fatima looked at her hands. They were cartoony, too: curved and with only four fingers. She didn't care that she was missing a finger, but seriously, where was her superhero costume? Where was her laser gun?

"What kind of comic *is* this?!" Fatima asked.

"The best comic strip in the newspaper, of course: *Silly Willy!*"

The harsh truth dawned on Fatima. She wasn't in one of her favorite comic *books*, she was in a comic *strip*. Didn't a djinn know the difference? (Probably not. Comic books are relatively new compared to ancient mystical wish-granters.) And worse, it was the same lame comic strip old people used to giggle at in the Sunday newspaper.

In this comic, there were no robots or dragons or mutants or ninja assassins. There were no superheroes or cyborgs or vampires or werewolves or transforming machines from another world. There were no cryoprisons or black holes or spaceships or intergalactic jailbreaks. There were no mech battles or zombie warriors or mythical beasts or mystical archvillains or demon slayers or creature hunters or anything that was even remotely cool.

The only thing the *Silly Willy* comic strip offered was something much, much worse... *weekly life lessons*.

As Fatima screamed, "NOOOOOO!" the letters *N-O-O-O-O-O-O-!* appeared above her in a speech bubble.

CHAPTER 24
Mya & Madison

It was long past lunchtime, and the students of Classroom 13 were getting hungry. "I'm starving!" Teo moaned.

"We're more starving," Mya said.

"Yeah, we're twins, which means we're *twice* as hungry," Madison agreed.

Mya & Madison were twins. The two identical sisters had the same exact hair, the same exact clothes, and often the same exact thoughts. So when it was their turn with the ~~genie~~ djinn, they said the same exact wish at the same exact time.

"We wish for a lifetime supply of pizza—with extra cheese and anchovies!" Madison & Mya said.

"*Two* girls using only *one* wish?" The Grand Djinn shrugged. "Sure makes my job easier! Wish granted!"

When Mya & Madison got home, they found stacks of pizza boxes all over their front lawn. They grabbed the first box, opened it, and breathed in the delicious smell of fresh pizza.

They ate slice after slice of anchovy-and-extra-cheese pizza until it was time for bed. They woke up and had some more for a midnight snack. They even ate it cold for breakfast the next morning (which is—let's be honest—the best way to eat pizza).

After a few days, Mya & Madison discovered they were tired of eating pizza. "I...I don't think I want another slice," Madison said.

"Me either," Mya said.

"Oh no! You are going to keep eating until all this pizza is gone!" their parents said. "You wished it; you eat it!"

But there were pizza boxes everywhere. The kitchen had boxes to the ceiling. The living room had so many pizza pies you couldn't find the couch. Both Madison & Mya's matching bedrooms were full. Luckily, the house was air-conditioned.

But the pizzas outside—under the hot sun all day long—began to stink. The stench attracted seagulls from miles away (along with one mallard that looked like their friend Mark).

The neighbors complained about the smell—not to mention the bird poop on their cars from all the nasty seagulls.

Mya & Madison tried their best to eat more pizza, but it was more than they could stomach. They ate slice after slice until they made themselves sick.

"Let's give it away," their parents suggested. "We'll have a neighborhood pizza party and give it away for free."

"It will give me gas," one neighbor said.

"This is just unsanitary," a second neighbor added.

"Why'd you have to wish for anchovies? Who does that?!" the family next door asked. No one wanted the stinky old fish pizza.

Soon, the pizza began to mold and rot. More seagulls came, and cockroaches, too. Some people even said they'd seen a certain "Pizza Rat" arrive in town on a flight from New York City.

The neighbors formed an angry mob, but instead of pitchforks, they came waving regular forks around. (I guess it was supposed to be symbolic.) They demanded Madison & Mya find a way to destroy the remaining pizza slices. They didn't know what was worse—how much the town hated them, or how terrible the rotten pizzas smelled.

Mya & Madison hid from the world behind a wall of pizza boxes. They drank pink stomach medicine and wished they'd been smart enough to each keep a second wish instead of doubling down on just one. If they still had it, they would make the same exact wish—they'd wish to *never* eat or see or smell pizza ever again.

CHAPTER 25
Preeya

Preeya didn't like the idea of just *one* wish. She didn't like one of anything—she always wanted more.

Her family and friends knew that Preeya could be a little greedy sometimes. On her birthday, she couldn't just have one kind of birthday cake, she needed chocolate cake *and* vanilla cake *and* strawberry cake *and* ice-cream cake *and* a cookie cake *and* cupcakes.

Preeya's favorite word was "and." She always wanted more.

So now that she was face-to-face with the Grand Djinn, she didn't want to wish for one *measly* thing....

She wanted ALL THE THINGS!

So Preeya thought of something clever. Preeya smiled a wicked smile at the blue wish-maker and said, "I wish to have a huge birthday party *and* I want all the best presents *and* a new swimming pool *and* my own hotel to have a sleepover *and* all the clothes from my favorite store *and*..."

As Preeya kept going, the Grand Djinn saw through her trickery. She wasn't the first to try this stunt, and she wouldn't be the last. He shrugged. He wanted to see if she ran out of words or ran out of breath first.

"...*and* I want my favorite boy band to perform a private show for me *and* I want them to dedicate a song just to me *and* I want a diamond tiara *and* I want a bunch of dolphins *and* my own limo *and* the prettiest dress in the whole wide world *and* I want to be a princess *and*..."

Preeya started to get light-headed. She couldn't stop to breathe. She needed to keep going. "...*and* a real castle *and* a real royal wedding to a prince *and* another prince who wants to marry me even though I don't want to marry him *and* a horse-drawn carriage *and* two glass slippers *and* a new car for my sixteenth birthday *and* a chocolate-dipping fountain *and* more friends *and*..."

When Preeya stopped to take a breath, the djinn held his hand up to silence her. "*And* your wish is granted!"

Preeya was ecstatic. She couldn't wait for her one wish *for so many things* to come true. She turned around and stuck out her tongue at all the other students. She had fooled the djinn, who had fooled all the other students. Or so Preeya thought....

The djinn was the one smiling wickedly now. There was a *poof* of smoke. When it cleared, Preeya's face was pressed up against glass.

She looked outside and saw the rest of Classroom 13 and her fellow students staring down at her. The djinn had shrunk her and placed her inside a snow globe—along with everything else she had wished for.

It was a pity she asked for so much. With so many things, it was a painfully tight squeeze in there. Preeya could barely breathe.

"Mshhhhh...Llllinduhhhhh..." she tried to say, barely able to move her lips. "A lllittle helllllp, pplllleease...?"

Ms. Linda picked up Preeya's snow globe and placed it on her desk. It made a very nice paperweight.

CHAPTER 26
Ximena

Ximena had (what some people refer to as) the *travel bug*. This is just a weird way of saying Ximena liked to travel. There were no bugs involved.

Her family was poor, so they rarely went anywhere farther than the grocery store. In fact, Ximena had never left the town she was born in. She'd never even seen a different state.

With a global vacation in mind, Ximena told the ~~genie~~ djinn her desire: "I wish to take a trip around the world with my family."

The Grand Djinn snapped his blue fingers. Ximena and her entire family were magically transported onto a plane. They were thirty-nine thousand feet in the air, circling the globe.

"This is so exciting!" Ximena said, looking out the window at the clouds and ocean below. "Where are we going to land first?"

"We aren't," the flight attendant told her.

"What?!"

"This is Djinn Airlines. We're flying *around* the whole world—as you wished. We don't have a destination."

"But what about fuel?" Ximena asked, trying to think of any reason to get off the plane. "Eventually, we'll run out. We'll have to land to refuel, right?"

"Nope," the flight attendant said. "We have infinite fuel, infinite in-flight meals, infinite in-flight movies, and a nearly infinite wait to use the bathroom. Just like a real airline."

Ximena's family's smiles turned into frowns. They buckled in for the longest flight of their lives. They dined on peanuts, pretzels, and the same egg salad sandwiches for breakfast, lunch, and dinner every day for days. The air in the cabin always had the odor of a recycled fart. And true to the flight attendant's word, they never landed.

The plane just kept circling the globe. Ximena thought she saw a few famous sites but she couldn't be sure—everything looked ant-sized from this high up in the sky.

When she got bored, she watched an in-flight movie. Ironically, *Aladdin* was playing on every channel. When she got tired, Ximena slept (uncomfortably) sitting up. She realized she should have requested to fly first class. Coach was horrible.

When she had to go, *you know*, she waited

her turn, doing the *I need to pee* dance until her bladder felt like it would explode. And the bathrooms? Let's just say sharing the bathroom with two hundred people on a very long flight gets very, very gross.

It was a trip Ximena would never forget.

CHAPTER 27
Jacob

Jacob loves TV. When he isn't at school, he's binge-watching his favorite shows. If he's not viewing them on an actual television, he's watching them on his tablet or his phone or his computer. He even has a waterproof TV setup in the bathtub so he can stream shows in the shower.

(By the way, I do *not* recommend having a

tablet anywhere near your bathtub. Never mind the possibility of electrocution, tablets are very expensive. And stores will *not* accept "innocent bath-time accident" as a reason for return, no matter how much I—I mean, *you*—whine or cry or pitch a tantrum. Trust me.)

Anyhoo. When Jacob's turn to make a wish came, he said, "I wish to be a TV star!"

Instead of just quickly granting the wish, the Grand Djinn paused to think. (Apparently, the blue man knew all about making Hollywood dreams come true.)

"What kind of star?" the djinn asked. "The party-all-the-time kind? The fat-sad-former-child-star kind? Or the mega-famous-superstar kind?"

"Mega-famous-superstar, please," Jacob said.

So the djinn made Jacob famous. Mega-super famous.

How famous *is* mega-super famous?

Well, as soon as the magic dust cleared, an army of paparazzi appeared. Paparazzi—also known as terrible and devious photographers who will do anything to snap a photo—started snapping his photo. The camera flashes were blinding.

Jacob ran out of Classroom 13, out of the school, and toward home. The paparazzi chased him. When he fell, they snapped pictures of him and said, "Celebrity klutz! Great headline!" Jacob was lucky his ankle wasn't broken.

He finally managed to hide behind Mrs. Crabapple's house. Her laundry was hanging up in her backyard, and he hid behind a giant dress. Looking up, he realized he was surrounded by ladies underwear. "Ack!" he gasped, and made a run for it.

But when he got home, there was no way to get in. His house was mobbed by legions of adoring fans. Every time a car passed by, his fans screamed in excitement, thinking it was him. These fans called themselves "Ja-Cubs for Jacob." The Ja-Cubs had handmade signs and shirts that read JACOB IS MY HERO, or JA-CUB 4 LYFE, or JACOB, WILL YOU MARRY ME?!

Jacob was hiding across the street, trying to figure out how to get into his house unnoticed.

Hours and hours passed. Finally, the Ja-Cubs set up tents and sleeping bags and went to sleep. Very carefully, he tiptoed between the snoring fans and snuck into his own house.

Is this what stars live through every day? Jacob wondered. *It's exhausting.* At least it felt good to be home, away from the craziness of new famousness.

That's when his parents turned on the light and surprised him by giving him a hug. (You see, Jacob's parents were usually rather private and antisocial parents. They mumbled maybe one or two words to him each month. It was usually "no.")

"Hi, honey. Why are you home so early?" his mom asked.

"Early? It's after midnight!" Jacob said, surprised he wasn't grounded.

"Son, you're a mega-famous superstar. You should be at work right now," his dad said.

"Work?!"

"Of course. All mega-famous superstars work twenty-three hours a day. That's how they stay famous."

"I don't want to work that much!" Jacob cried. "When will I watch TV?!"

"TV? Oh, sweetie." His parents giggled. "Mega-famous superstars don't watch TV. They don't have time. They're too busy being *on* TV."

Jacob fell to his knees dramatically and screamed, "NOOOOOOOOOOOOOO!"

CHAPTER 28
Ethan

To no one's surprise, Ethan didn't know what to wish for yet. This was because Ethan was always "of two minds" about everything. As soon as he started to make a choice (for example, picking Swiss cheese over cheddar cheese), he'd convince himself to change his mind. (Cheddar was clearly better; it was sharper!) Then he'd change it again. (No, it's too sharp! Swiss is subtle. Swiss all the way!)

This may seem nutty to you and me, but it was totally normal for Ethan. It was just how his brain worked—he liked debating things.

Ethan was happy to be at the back of the wish line. He needed extra time to weigh his wishing options.

So—while you've been reading this whole time, and his classmates have been making their wishes—Ethan has been arguing with himself at the back of the line trying to decide what to wish for.

I love sports. Perhaps I should wish to own all the football teams in the world. Then I could watch the games anytime I'd want and I'd be stinking rich. Then again, I prefer baseball....Then again, it would be cool to own Super Bowl Sundays. Then again, baseball is America's favorite pastime....

And so on and on it went in Ethan's head.

When it came time for Ethan to make his wish, he still hadn't made up his mind. The Grand Djinn grew more impatient by the second.

"Hurry up. I need a nap. It's been a long day of wish granting."

"I'm sorry, I'm sorry! Just, uh, I think, um..." Ethan stuttered. Finally, he blurted out, *"Ugh, I wish I could think of something!"*

"Wish granted!" the Grand Djinn said.

Just then, an idea popped into Ethan's head—the perfect wish.

Though what that wish is, we will never know.

"Okay, I know what to wish for!" Ethan exclaimed.

"Nuh-uh, man," the Grand Djinn said, shaking his head. "You just used your wish to wish for an idea. Next!"

Ethan drove his wheelchair to the wall so he could bang his head on it. He was furious with himself for having been so careless.

No, he wasn't mad. He was sad.

No, mad, he thought. *I'm mad. Well...maybe*

more sad. But why was the djinn so literal? That makes me mad! I used up my wish on a technicality. No more wish. That makes me sad. No...it makes me mad!

The great sad-versus-mad debate would continue for several days—until Ethan had a new idea about how to get his wish back....

CHAPTER 29

Olivia

"**I** wish for world peace," Olivia said.

"What?!" The djinn was shocked by Olivia's wish. "That wish isn't selfish at all. No one ever wishes for that. It's so...so...*selfless*!"

"Not really," Olivia said. "I am the smartest student in school. I know better than to waste my wish on something silly. I needed to make a wish that I can put on my future college applications that will help me get accepted at the best schools."

"Well played," the djinn said. He snapped his fingers, and—miraculously—all war and violence and anger vanished from the earth.

CHAPTER 30
Second-Chance Santiago

Days went by, and the students of Classroom 13 were—for the most part—very miserable. They'd had a chance at making a wish (*any wish!*), and somehow they each had screwed it up.

Well, except for Mason. He loved his flashlight. And Earl, who loved his sunflower seeds.

Oh, and of course, Olivia. She wished for

114

world peace. And the whole world was at peace.

After several days, Ethan had finally thought of a plan to get his wish back....Ethan snuck out his cell phone and texted Santiago:

DUDE. R u still sick?

a djinn is here granting wishes. he was gonna leave but Ms. L insisted you get your wish first.

Get here ASAP.

B rite there!

A few minutes later, Santiago Santos appeared in the doorway of Classroom 13. He was over the flu, but now he had strep throat. With a runny nose and puffy face, and still wearing his bathrobe, Santiago dragged himself to the front of the class and picked up the djinn's lamp. He gave it a rub.

"Who's this?" the Grand Djinn asked.

"I'm Santia—*cough*!" After a phlegmy coughing fit, he continued. "I rode my bike all the way here so I could make my wish."

"Sorry, pal," the Grand Djinn said. "I'm finished granting wishes to this classroom full of weirdos."

"Weird? Who's weird?" Liam asked through his fishbowl.

"What a rude djinn!" Ms. Linda said. "That's the last time I bring a strange lamp into class."

"Come on!" Santiago begged. "One last wish, please?!"

"You weren't here when Ms. Linda rubbed my lamp," the djinn said. "So no wish for you."

"No wish?! *Ugh*. I wish I'd been here that

day!" Santiago said, accidentally rubbing the other lamp on Ms. Linda's desk with his butt.

In a burst of golden light, Ava the Djinn appeared. "Hey, Santi! Still sick, huh? Shoulda wished to be healthy, but I'll grant your wish."

"What wish?" Santiago asked.

"You just wished you'd been here that day. And your wish is my command!"

Ava snapped her fingers. Suddenly, time began to go *backward*!

All of Classroom 13's wishes were undone: Ximena's family found themselves off the plane and back home. Emma's parents were divorced (and happy) again. Ava was no longer a ~~genie~~ djinn, and Mark shed his feathers.

Unfortunately, even Olivia's wish was undone. No more world peace. See ya later, world peace! (Hopefully...but probably not.)

It was as if the last few days had never happened at all—except that everyone remembered.

Everyone and everything was back to the way it had been—except Santiago was in class that morning, despite being sick. Santiago sniffled.

Even Ms. Linda's swollen lip was back. She winced from the bee sting. "Aww gweat, my wip is swowwen again!"

This was Ethan's chance to redo his wish—his plan had worked. He shouted to the class, "Okay, this time, let's all think hard on our wishes before Ms. Linda rubs the lamp for the first time. We can all have new wishes!"

The whole class cheered. It was almost too perfect.

As Ms. Linda picked up the lamp, Santiago let out a horrific and loud snot-filled sneeze that startled everyone. *"ACCCHHHOOOOOOO!"* It scared Ms. Linda so bad, she dropped the djinn's lamp, and it shattered on the floor into a million pieces.

The djinn shouted, "I'm free!" and flew away.

★   ★   ★

The rest of the do-over day was just like any other day.

For the kids, it was a long stretch of *wishing* for the bell to ring.

For Ms. Linda, it was a long wait of *wishing* for some topical cream to numb her throbbing lip.

And for the 13th Classroom, it was a long eternity of *wishing* someone, anyone, could hear it. But the Classroom only spoke at a whisper. That's why no one heard it begging for a chance to ask the djinn for a wish.

It would've wished for the one thing it wanted most in the world—but that's a tale for another time.

CHAPTER 31
Your Chapter

That's right—it's your turn!

Grab some paper and a writing utensil. (Not a fork, silly. Try a pencil or pen.) Or if you have one of those fancy computer doo-hickeys, use that. Now tell me...

If *YOU* had one magic wish, what would *YOU* wish for?!

When you're done, share it with your teacher, your family, and your friends. (Don't forget your pets! Pets like to hear stories, too.) You can even ask your parents to send me your chapter at the address below.

HONEST LEE

LITTLE, BROWN BOOKS FOR YOUNG READERS

1290 Avenue of the Americas

New York, NY 10104

Don't Miss Book 3!

Available soon!